FIRESIDE STORIES

*She put on her teeny-tiny bonnet and went out
of her teeny-tiny house to take a teeny-tiny walk.*

FIRESIDE STORIES

Selected and
Edited by
VERONICA S.
HUTCHINSON

With drawings
by LOIS LENSKI

MINTON, BALCH & COMPANY
New York

BY

MPANY

Eleventh Impression

Printed in the United States of America

To
MARGARET CARROLL DAVIS

ACKNOWLEDGMENTS

The editor wishes to thank the following for permission to use stories listed:

The Century Company for "The Foolish Timid Rabbit" from "Jataka Tales," retold by Ellen C. Babbitt.

Frederick A. Stokes Company for "The Straw Ox and the Hungry Wolf" from "More Russian Picture Tales" by Valery Carrick, and for "The Jackal and the Alligator" from Darton's "Wonder Books of Beasts."

Harper & Brothers for "The Wonderful Pot" from Day's "Danish Fairy Tales."

Dodd, Mead & Company for "The Hare and the Hedgehog" from "Little Brother and Sister."

G. P. Putnam's Sons for "The Kettle That Would Not Walk" from Joseph Jacobs' "More English Fairy Tales."

All of these have been slightly adapted.

CONTENTS

ILLUSTRATIONS

Full pages in color

Full pages in black and white

And many other smaller illustrations in black and white

Teeny-Tiny

NCE upon a time there was a teeny-tiny woman who lived in a teeny-tiny village. One day this teeny-tiny woman put on her teeny-tiny bonnet and went out of her teeny-tiny house to take a teeny-tiny walk. And when the teeny-tiny woman had gone a teeny-tiny way she came to a teeny-tiny gate; and the teeny-tiny woman opened the teeny-tiny gate and went into a teeny-tiny field. And when the teeny-tiny woman had gone into the teeny-tiny field she saw a teeny-tiny bone under a teeny-tiny tree, and the teeny-tiny woman said to her teeny-tiny self, "This teeny-tiny bone will make me

some teeny-tiny soup for my teeny-tiny supper."

So the teeny-tiny woman put the teeny-tiny bone into her teeny-tiny pocket and went home to her teeny-tiny house. And when the teeny-tiny woman got home to her teeny-tiny house she was a teeny-tiny tired, and she went up her teeny-tiny stairs to her teeny-tiny chamber and put the teeny-tiny bone into a teeny-tiny cupboard. Then she went to sleep in her teeny-tiny bed, and when she had been asleep

a teeny-tiny time she was awakened by a teeny-tiny voice from the teeny-tiny cupboard which said:—

"Give me my bone!"

And the teeny-tiny woman was a teeny-tiny frightened. So she hid her teeny-tiny head under the teeny-tiny clothes and went to sleep again. And when she had been asleep for a teeny-tiny time, the teeny-

4

tiny voice cried out again from the teeny-tiny cupboard a teeny-tiny louder:—

"Give me my bone!"

This made the teeny-tiny woman a teeny-tiny

more frightened. So she hid her teeny-tiny head a teeny-tiny farther under the teeny-tiny clothes.

And when the teeny-tiny woman had been asleep again a teeny-tiny time, the teeny-tiny voice from the teeny-tiny cupboard said again a teeny-tiny louder:—

"Give me my bone!"

And the teeny-tiny woman was a teeny-tiny more frightened; but she put her teeny-tiny head out of the teeny-tiny clothes and said in her loudest teeny-tiny voice:—

"TAKE IT!"

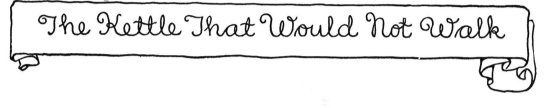

The Kettle That Would Not Walk

NE day a Gotham man was getting ready to go to market, and his wife said to him, "Husband, we need a new iron kettle for the fireplace. Don't fail to buy one."

So the man bought a kettle at Nottingham, and toward evening he took it on his arm and started for home. But the kettle was heavy, and at length his arm grew tired with carrying it and he set it down. While he was resting he noticed that the kettle had three legs.

"What a pity that I did not see those legs before!"

cried the man. "Here you have three legs and I have but two, and yet I have been carrying you. 'T were fairer that you had carried me. Well, you shall take me the rest of the way, at least."

Then he seated himself in the kettle and said, "Now, go on; I am all ready;" but the kettle stood stock still on its three legs and would not move.

"Ah!" said the man, "you are stubborn, are you? You want me to keep on carrying you, I suppose; but I shall not. I will tell you the way and you can stay where you are until you get ready to follow me."

So he told the kettle where he lived and how to get there, and then off the man went. When he reached home his wife asked him where the kettle was.

"Oh, it will be along in good time," he replied.

10

When he reached home his wife asked him where the kettle was.

"And what do you mean by that?" said she.

"Why," said he, "the kettle I bought has three legs, and was better able to walk here from Nottingham market than I who have but two legs. Yet I never noticed it had legs until I was nearly here. Then I told it to walk the rest of the way itself, for I would carry it no farther."

"Where did you leave it?" asked the wife.

"You need not be anxious," responded the man. "I told it the way, and it will be along in good time, as I said before."

"And where did you leave it?" again asked the wife.

"At Gotham bridge," he replied.

She was not so sure about its coming as he was and she hurried off to get it. When she brought it home the man said, "I am glad you have it safe, wife, for I have been thinking while you were gone that it might have taken a notion to walk back to Nottingham if we had left it alone there in the road much longer."

Titty Mouse and Tatty Mouse

Titty Mouse and Tatty Mouse

TITTY MOUSE and Tatty Mouse both lived in a house. Titty Mouse went a-leasing and Tatty Mouse went a-leasing; so they both went a-leasing. Titty Mouse leased an ear of corn, and Tatty Mouse leased an ear of corn; so they both leased an ear of corn. Titty Mouse made a pudding, and Tatty Mouse made a pudding; so they both made a pudding. And Tatty Mouse put her pudding into the pot to boil, but when Titty went to put hers in, the pot tumbled over, and scalded her to death.

Then Tatty sat down and wept; then a three-legged stool said, "Tatty, why do you weep?"

"Titty's dead," said Tatty, "and so I weep."

17

"Then," said the stool, "I'll hop;" so the stool hopped.

Then the broom in the corner of the room said: "Stool, why do you hop?"

"Oh," said the stool, "Titty's dead, and Tatty weeps, and so I hop."

"Then," said the broom, "I'll sweep;" so the broom began to sweep.

Then said the door, "Broom, why do you sweep?"

"Oh," said the broom, "Titty's dead, and Tatty weeps, and the stool hops, and so I sweep!"

"Then," said the door, "I'll jar;" so the door jarred.

Then said the window, "Door, why do you jar?"

"Oh," said the door, "Titty's dead, and Tatty weeps, the stool hops, and the broom sweeps, and so I jar!"

"Then," said the window, "I'll creak;" so the window creaked.

Now there was an old form outside the house, and when the window creaked, the form said: "Window, why do you creak?"

"Oh!" said the window, "Titty's dead, and Tatty weeps, and the stool hops, and the broom sweeps, the door jars, and so I creak!"

"Then," said the old form, "I'll run round the house;" so the old form ran round the house.

Now there was a fine large walnut tree growing by the cottage, and the tree said to the form: "Form, why do you run round the house?"

"Oh," said the form, "Titty's dead, and Tatty weeps, and the stool hops, and the broom sweeps, the door jars, and the window creaks, and so I run round the house."

"Then," said the walnut tree, "I'll shed my leaves;" so the walnut tree shed its beautiful green leaves.

Now there was a little bird perched on one of the boughs of the tree, and when all the leaves fell, it said: "Walnut tree, why do you shed your leaves?"

"Oh," said the tree, "Titty's dead, and Tatty weeps, the stool hops, and the broom sweeps, the door jars, and the window creaks, the old form runs round the house, and so I shed my leaves!"

"Then," said the little bird, "I'll moult all my feathers;" so he moulted all his pretty feathers.

Now there was a little girl walking below, carrying a jug of milk for her brothers' and sisters' sup-

"Little bird, why do you moult all your feathers?"

per, and when she saw the poor little bird moult all his feathers, she said: "Little bird, why do you moult all your feathers?"

"Oh," said the little bird, "Titty's dead, and Tatty

weeps, the stool hops, the broom sweeps, the door jars, and the window creaks, the old form runs round the house, the walnut tree sheds its leaves, and so I moult all my feathers."

"Then," said the little girl, "I'll spill the milk;" so she dropped the pitcher and spilt the milk.

Now there was an old man just by on the top of a ladder thatching a rick, and when he saw the little girl spill the milk, he said: "Little girl, what do you mean by spilling the milk?—your little brothers and sisters must go without their supper."

"Oh," said the little girl, "Titty's dead, and Tatty weeps, the stool hops, and the broom sweeps, the door jars, and the window creaks, the old form runs round the house, the walnut tree sheds all its leaves, the little bird moults all its feathers, and so I spill the milk!"

"Oh," said the old man, "then I'll tumble off the ladder and break my neck;" so he tumbled off the ladder and broke his neck; and when the old man broke his neck, the great walnut tree fell down with a crash and upset the old form and house, and the house falling knocked the window out, and the window knocked the door down, and the door upset the broom, and the broom upset the stool, and poor little Tatty Mouse was buried beneath the ruins.

Why the Bear is Stumpy-tailed

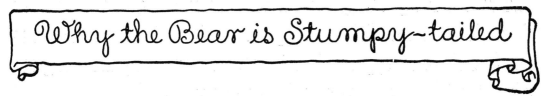

Why the Bear is Stumpy-tailed

NE day the Bear met the Fox, who came slinking along with a string of fish he had stolen.

"Whence did you get those? asked the Bear.

"Oh! my Lord Bruin, I've been out fishing and caught them," said the Fox.

So the Bear had a mind to learn to fish too, and bade the Fox tell him how he was to set about it.

"Oh, it's an easy craft for you," answered the Fox, "and soon learnt. You've only got to go upon the ice, and cut a hole and stick your tail down into it; and so you must go on holding it there as long as you can. You're not to mind if your tail smarts a little; that's when the fish bite. The longer you hold it there the more fish you'll get; and then all at once out with it, with a cross pull sideways, and with a strong pull too."

Yes; the Bear did as the Fox had said, and held

25

his tail a long, long time down in the hole, till it was fast frozen in. Then he pulled it out with a cross pull, and it snapped short off. That's why Bruin goes about with a stumpy tail to this very day.

The Bear had a mind to learn to fish too.

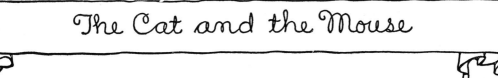

The Cat and the Mouse

The Cat and the Mouse

 HE cat and the mouse
     Play'd in the malt-house:
     The cat bit the mouse's tail off.
     "Pray, puss, give me my tail."
      "No," said the cat, "I'll not give
you your tail, till you go to the cow,
and fetch me some milk."

First she leapt, and then she ran,
Till she came to the cow, and thus began:

    "Pray, Cow, give me milk, that I may give cat milk,
that cat may give me my own tail again."

    "No," said the cow, "I will give you no milk, till
you go to the farmer, and get me some hay."

First she leapt, and then she ran,
Till she came to the farmer and thus began:

31

"Pray, Farmer, give me hay, that I may give cow hay, that cow may give me milk, that I may give cat milk, that cat may give me my own tail again."

"No," said the farmer, "I'll give you no hay, till you go to the butcher and fetch me some meat."

First she leapt, and then she ran,
Till she came to the butcher, and thus began:

"Pray, Butcher, give me meat, that I may give farmer meat, that farmer may give me hay, that I may give cow hay, that cow may give me milk, that I may give cat milk, that cat may give me my own tail again."

"No," said the butcher, "I'll give you no meat, till you go to the baker and fetch me some bread."

"Pray, Cow, give me some milk!"

First she leapt, and then she ran,
Till she came to the baker, and thus began:

"Pray, Baker, give me bread, that I may give butcher bread, that butcher may give me meat, that I may give farmer meat, that farmer may give me hay, that I may give cow hay, that cow may give me milk, that I may give cat milk, that cat may give me my own tail again."

"Yes," said the baker, "I'll give you some bread,
But if you eat my meal, I'll cut off your head."

Then the baker gave mouse bread, and mouse gave butcher bread, and butcher gave mouse meat, and mouse gave farmer meat, and farmer gave mouse hay, and mouse gave cow hay, and cow gave mouse milk, and mouse gave cat milk, and cat gave mouse her own tail again.

The Hungry Wolf

The Hungry Wolf

THERE was once a wolf, and as he was very hungry, he went to see what he could find for dinner. After a bit he saw a ram feeding in a meadow, so he went up to him and said: "Mr. Ram, Mr. Ram, I'm going to eat you!"

But the ram answered: "Who are you, I should like to know, that you mean to eat me?"

"I'm a wolf, and I'm looking for a good dinner," said the wolf.

"What sort of wolf do you fancy you are?" answered the ram. "You're not; you're a dog!"

"No, I'm not a dog," said he. "I'm a wolf."

"Well, then," answered the ram, "if you're a wolf, stand at the bottom of the hill and open your jaws wide. Then I'll run down the hill and jump straight into your mouth."

"All right," said the wolf.

So he stood at the bottom of the hill and opened

37

his mouth wide, while the ram climbed to the top of the hill. Then he ran down the hill very fast, and hit the wolf with his horns as hard as he could.

The wolf rolled over knocked senseless with the blow, while the ram ran off home. And there lay the wolf, till at last he came to himself again, with all his bones aching.

"Well, how foolish I must have been!" thought he. "Who ever saw a ram jump into one's mouth of his own free will?"

Then he went on further, just as hungry as ever, and after a bit he saw a horse walking in a meadow nibbling grass.

So he went up to him and said: "Mr. Horse, Mr. Horse, I'm going to eat you!"

But the horse answered: "Who are you, I should like to know, that you mean to eat me?"

"I'm a wolf."

"You think again," answered the horse. "You're only a dog."

"No, I'm not a dog," said he. "I'm a wolf."

"Oh, if you are sure you're a wolf, it's all right. Only as I'm not very fat yet, you'd better begin on my tail, and meanwhile I'll be munching some more grass and get a little fuller."

So the wolf went up to him from behind, and was just going to get to work on his tail, when the horse let out at him as hard as he could! And the wolf rolled over, while the horse ran off.

And there sat the wolf, and he thought, "Well, wasn't I a foolish one! Whoever heard of anyone starting to eat a horse by the tail?"

And so he wandered on further, when after a bit he saw a pig coming towards him. When he got to him he said : "Mr. Pig, Mr. Pig, I'm going to eat you!"

But the pig answered: "Who are you, I should like to know, that you mean to eat me?"

"I'm a wolf."

"You're a queer sort of wolf," answered the pig. "You're only a dog!"

"No, I'm not a dog," said he. "I'm a wolf!"

"Oh, that's all right then," answered the pig, "you just sit down on my back. I'll give you a ride and then you can eat me."

So the wolf sat down on the pig's back, when lo and behold! the pig carried him straight into the village.

And all the dogs ran out, made a dash for the wolf, and began to tease him. And they teased him so much, it was all he could do to tear himself away and run off back into the forest.

The Foolish Timid Rabbit

The Foolish Timid Rabbit

O NCE upon a time, a little Rabbit was sound asleep under a big palm tree.

All at once he woke up, and thought: "What if the world should break up! What then would become of me?"

At that moment some Monkeys dropped a cocoanut. It fell down on the ground just back of the Rabbit.

Hearing the noise, the Rabbit said to himself: "The earth is all breaking up!"

He jumped up and ran as fast as he could, without even looking back to see what made the noise.

Another Rabbit saw him running, and called after him, "What are you running so fast for?"

"Don't ask me!" he cried.

But the other Rabbit ran after him, begging to know what was the matter.

Then the first Rabbit said: "Don't you know? The earth is all breaking up!"

And on he ran, and the second Rabbit ran with him.

The next Rabbit they met ran with them when he heard the earth was all breaking up.

One Rabbit after another joined them, until there were hundreds of Rabbits running as fast as they could go.

They passed a Deer, calling out to him that the earth was all breaking up. The Deer then ran with them.

The Deer called to a Fox to come along because the earth was all breaking up.

On and on they ran, and an Elephant joined them.

At last the Lion saw the animals running, and heard their cry that the earth was all breaking up.

He thought there must be some mistake, so he ran to the foot of the hill in front of them and roared three times.

This stopped them, for they knew the voice of the

King of Beasts, and they feared him.

"Why are you running so fast?" asked the Lion.

"Oh, King Lion," they answered him, "the earth is all breaking up!"

"Who saw it breaking up?" asked the Lion.

"I didn't," said the Fox.

"The Rabbits told me about it," said the Deer.

One after another of the Rabbits said: "I did not see it, but another Rabbit told me about it."

At last the Lion came to the Rabbit who had first said the earth was all breaking up.

"Is it true that the earth is all breaking up?" the Lion asked.

"Yes, O Lion, it is," said the Rabbit. "I was asleep under a palm tree. I woke up and thought, 'What would become of me if the earth should all break up?' At that very moment, I heard the sound of the earth breaking up, and I ran away."

"Then," said the Lion, "you and I will go back to the place where the earth began to break up, and see what is the matter."

So the Lion put the little Rabbit on his back, and away they went like the wind. The other animals waited for them at the foot of the hill.

The Rabbit told the Lion when they were near the place where he slept, and the Lion saw just where the Rabbit had been sleeping.

He saw, too, the cocoanut that had fallen to the ground near by. Then the Lion said to the Rabbit, "It must have been the sound of the cocoanut fall-

ing to the ground that you heard. You foolish Rabbit!"

And the Lion ran back to the other animals, and
told them all about it.

If it had not been for the wise King of Beasts,
they might be running still.

Drakestail

RAKESTAIL was very little, that is why he was called Drakestail; but tiny as he was he had brains, and he knew what he was about; for having begun with nothing he ended by saving a hundred crowns. Now the king of the country, who was very extravagant and never kept any money, having heard that Drakestail had some, went one day in his own person to borrow his hoard, and, my word, in those days Drakestail was not a little proud of having lent money to the king.

But after the first and second year, seeing that the king never even dreamed of paying the interest, he became uneasy, so much so that at last he resolved to go and see his majesty and ask for his money.

So one fine morning Drakestail, very spruce and fresh, took the road, singing: "Quack, quack, quack, when shall I get my money back?"

He had not gone far when he met friend Fox, on his rounds that way.

"Good morning, neighbor," said the friend, "where are you off to so early?"

"I am going to the king for what he owes me."

"Oh, take me with thee!"

Drakestail said to himself: "One can't have too many friends."

Aloud said he, "I will, but going on all fours you will soon be tired. Make yourself quite small, get into my throat—go into my gizzard, and I will carry you."

"Happy thought!" said friend Fox.

He took bag and baggage, and, presto! was gone.

And Drakestail was off again, all spruce and fresh, still singing: "Quack, quack, quack, when shall I have my money back?"

He had not gone far when he met his lady friend Ladder, leaning on her wall.

"Good morning, my duckling," said the lady friend, "whither away so bold?"

"I am going to the king for what he owes me."

"Oh, take me with thee!"

Drakestail said to himself: "One can't have too many friends."

Aloud said he: "I will, but then with your wooden legs you will soon be tired. Make yourself quite small, get into my throat—go into my gizzard, and I will carry you."

"Happy thought," said friend Ladder, and nimble, bag and baggage, went to keep company with friend Fox.

"And, "Quack, quack, quack," Drakestail was off again, singing and spruce as before. A little further on he met his sweetheart, friend River, wandering quietly in the sunshine.

"Thou, my cherub," said she, "whither so lonesome, with arching tail on this muddy road?"

"I am going to the king, you know, for what he owes me."

"Oh, take me with thee!"

Drakestail said to himself: "One can't have too many friends."

Aloud said he: "I will, but you who sleep while you walk will soon get tired. Make yourself quite small, get into my throat—go into my gizzard, and I will carry you."

"Ah, happy thought!" said friend River.

She took bag and baggage, and glou, glou, glou, in she went between friend Fox and friend Ladder.

And, "Quack, quack, quack," Drakestail was off again singing.

A little further on he met Comrade Wasp's-nest, maneuvering his wasps.

"Well, good morning, friend Drakestail," said comrade Wasp's-nest, "Where are we bound for so spruce and fresh?"

"I am going to the king for what he owes me."

"Oh, take me with thee!"

Drakestail said to himself: "One can't have too many friends."

Aloud said he: "I will, but then with your battalion to drag along, you will soon be tired. Make yourself quite small, go into my throat—get into my gizzard, and I will carry you."

"By Jove! that's a good idea!" said comrade Wasp's-nest.

And left file! he took the same road to join the others with all his party. There was not much room, but by closing up a bit they managed. And Drakestail was off again singing.

He arrived thus at the capital, and threaded his way straight up the High Street still running and singing, "Quack, quack, quack, when shall I get my money back?" to the great astonishment of the good folks of the city, till he came to the king's palace.

He struck with the knocker: "Toc! toc!"

"Who is there?" asked the porter, putting his head out of the wicket.

"'Tis I, Drakestail. I wish to speak to the king."

"Speak to the king! That's easily said. The king is dining, and will not be disturbed."

"Tell him that it is I, and I have come he well knows why."

The porter shut his wicket and went up to tell it

to the king, who, surrounded by all his ministers, was just sitting down to dinner with a napkin round his neck.

He arrived thus at the capital, and threaded his way straight up the High Street.

"Good, good!" said the king laughing. "I know what it is! Make him come in, and put him with the turkeys and chickens."

The porter descended.

"Have the goodness to enter."

"Good!" said Drakestail to himself, "I shall now see how they eat at court."

"This way, this way," said the porter. "One step further. There, there you are."

"How? what? in the poultry-yard?"

Fancy how vexed Drakestail was!

"Ah! so that's it," said he. "Wait! I will compel you to receive me. Quack, quack, quack, when shall I get my money back?"

But turkeys and chickens are creatures who don't like people that are not as themselves. When they saw the newcomer and how he was made, and when they heard him crying too, they began to look black at him.

"What is it? What does he want?"

Finally they rushed at him all together, to over-whelm him with pecks.

"I am lost!" said Drakestail to himself, when by good luck he remembered his comrade friend Fox, and he cried:

"Reynard, Reynard, come out of your earth,
Or Drakestail's life is of little worth."

Then friend Fox, who was only waiting for these words, hastened out, threw himself on the wicked fowls, and quick! quack! at the end of five minutes

there was not one left alive. And Drakestail, quite content, began to sing again, "Quack, quack, quack, when shall I get my money back?"

When the king, who was still at table, heard this refrain, and the poultry-woman came to tell him what had been going on in the yard, he was terribly annoyed.

He ordered them to throw this tail of a Drake into the well, to make an end of him.

And it was done as he commanded. Drakestail was in despair of getting himself out of such a deep hole, when he remembered his lady friend Ladder.

"Ladder, Ladder, come out of thy hold,
  Or Drakestail's days will soon be told."

Friend Ladder, who was only waiting for these words, hastened out, leaned her two arms on the edge

of the well; then Drakestail climbed nimbly on her back, and hop! he was in the yard, where he began to sing louder than ever.

When the king, who was still at table and laughing at the good trick he had played on Drakestail, heard him again asking for his money, he became livid with rage.

He commanded that the furnace should be heated, and this tail of a Drake thrown into it, because he must be a sorcerer.

The furnace was soon hot, but this time Drakestail was not so afraid; he counted on his sweetheart, friend River.

"River, River, outward flow,
    Or to death Drakestail must go."

Friend River hastened out, and errouf! threw herself into the furnace, which she flooded, with all the people who had lighted it; after which she flowed growling into the hall of the palace to the height of more than four feet.

And Drakestail, quite content, began to swim, singing deafeningly, "Quack, quack, quack, when shall I get my money back?"

The king was still at table, and thought himself quite sure of his game; but when he heard Drakestail singing again, and when they told him all that had passed, he became furious and got up from the table brandishing his fists.

"Bring him here, and I'll put an end to him! Bring him here quickly!" cried he.

And quickly two footmen ran to fetch Drakestail.

"At last," said the poor chap, going up the great stairs, "they have decided to receive me."

Imagine his terror when on entering he saw the king as red as a turkey cock, and all his ministers at-

tending him standing sword in hand. He thought this time it was all up with him. Happily he remembered that there was still one remaining friend, and he cried with dying accents:

"Wasp's-nest, Wasp's-nest, make a sally,
   Or Drakestail nevermore may rally."

Hereupon the scene changed.

"Bs, bs, bayonet them!" The brave Wasp's-nest rushed out with all his wasps. They threw themselves on the infuriated king and his ministers, and stung them so fiercely in the face that they lost their heads and not knowing where to hide themselves they all jumped pell-mell from the window and broke their necks on the pavement.

Behold Drakestail much astonished, all alone in the big saloon and master of the field. He could not get over it.

Nevertheless, he remembered shortly why he had come to the palace, and improving the occasion, he set to work to hunt for his dear money. But in vain he rummaged in all the drawers; he found nothing; all had been spent.

And ferreting thus from room to room he came at last to the one with the throne in it. Feeling fatigued, he sat himself down on it to think over his adventure.

In the meanwhile the people found their king and his ministers with their feet in the air on the pavement. They went into the palace to find out what had happened. On entering the throne room, they saw that there was already some one on the royal seat. They broke out in cries of surprise and joy:

"The King is dead, long live the King!
Heaven has sent us down this thing."

Drakestail, who was no longer surprised at anything, received the acclamations of the people as if he had never done anything else all his life.

A few of them certainly murmured that a Drakestail would make a fine king; those who knew him replied that a knowing drakestail was a more worthy king than the spendthrift who was lying on the pavement. In short, they ran and took the crown off the head of the late king, and placed it on that of Drakestail, whom it fitted like wax.

Thus he became king.

"And now," said he after the ceremony, "ladies and gentlemen, let's go to supper. I AM so hungry."

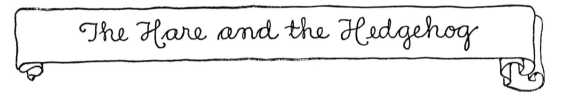

The Hare and the Hedgehog

The Hare and the Hedgehog

 NE Sunday morning about harvest time, just as the buckwheat was in bloom, the sun was shining brightly in the sky. The east wind was blowing warmly over the stubble-fields. The larks were singing in the air. The bees were buzzing among the buckwheat. The people were all going in their Sunday clothes to church, and all creatures were happy. And the hedgehog was happy too.

Well, he was standing by his door with his arms akimbo, enjoying the morning breezes, and slowly humming a little song to himself, which was neither better nor worse than the songs that hedgehogs usually do sing on a blessed Sunday morning. As thus he was singing half aloud to himself, it suddenly occurred to him that, while his wife was washing and drying the children, he might well take a walk into the field and see how his turnips were going on. Really, the turnips were not his at all, but they grew just

67

around the corner, and as he and his family were in the habit of helping themselves, he looked upon them as his own. No sooner said than done.

The hedgehog shut the house door behind him, and took the path to the field. He had not gone very far from home, and was just turning round a bush to go up into the turnip field, when he came across the hare, who had gone out on business of the same kind, namely, to visit his cabbages. When the hedgehog caught sight of the hare he bade him a friendly good morning. But the hare, who was in his own way a distinguished gentleman, and exceedingly haughty, did not return the hedgehog's greeting, but said to him in a most unfriendly manner, "How do you happen to be running about here in the field so early in the morning?"

"I am taking a walk," said the hedgehog.

"A walk!" said the hare, with a smile. "It seems to me you might use your legs for a better purpose."

This answer made the hedgehog furiously angry, for he can bear anything but a remark about his legs, because they are crooked by nature. So he replied, "You seem to imagine that you can do more with your legs than I can with mine."

"That is just what I can do," said the hare.

"That can be put to a test," said the hedgehog. "I wager that if we run a race, I will beat you."

"Oh, nonsense! You, with your short legs!" said the hare. 'Though, for my part, I'm willing, if you are so anxious for it. What shall we wager?"

"A golden turnip," said the hedgehog.

"Done," said the hare. "Shake hands on it and it may as well come off at once."

"Nay," said the hedgehog, "there is no such great hurry! I am still fasting. I will go home first and have a little breakfast. In half an hour I'll be back again at this place."

Hereupon the hedgehog departed, for the hare was quite satisfied with this. On his way the hedgehog thought to himself, "The hare relies on his long legs, but I will contrive to get the better of him. He may be a great man, but he is a very silly fellow, and he shall pay for what he has said."

So when the hedgehog reached home, he said to his wife, "Wife, dress yourself quickly; you must go to the field with me."

"What's going on now, then?" said his wife.

"I've made a wager with the hare. I am to run a race, and you must be present."

"Good heavens, husband," his wife cried. "Are you not right in your mind? Have you completely lost your wits? What can make you want to run a race with the hare?"

"Hold your tongue, woman," said the hedgehog; "that is my affair. Don't begin to discuss things

70

which are matters for men. Be off, and get ready to come with me."

What could the hedgehog's wife do? She had to obey him, whether she liked it or not.

So when they had set out on their way together, the hedgehog said to his wife, "Now pay attention to what I am going to say. Look you, I will make the long field our race course. The hare shall run in one furrow, and I in another, and we will begin the race from the top. Now all that you have to do is to place yourself here at the bottom, in the furrow, and when the hare reaches the end of his furrow alongside of you, you must cry out to him, 'Here I am already.'"

They reached the field, and the hedgehog showed his wife her place, and then walked up the field. When he reached the top, the hare was already there.

"Shall we start?" said the hare.

"Certainly," said the hedgehog.

"Then both together." So saying, each placed himself in his own furrow.

The hare counted, "One, two, three, and away!" and went off like a whirlwind down the field. The hedge-hog, however, only ran about three paces, and then he stooped down in the furrow, and stayed quietly where he was.

So when the hare at top speed reached the lower end of the field, the hedgehog's wife met him with the cry, "Here I am already!"

The hare was overcome with astonishment, for he thought it could but be the hedgehog himself who was calling to him, for the hedgehog's wife looked just like her husband.

The hare, however, thought to himself, "It can't have been done fairly," and cried, "It must be run again, let us have it again."

And once more he went off like wind in a storm, so that he seemed to fly. But the hedgehog's wife stayed quietly in her place. So when the hare reached the top of the hill, the hedgehog himself cried out to him, "Here I am already!"

The hare was quite beside himself with anger, and cried, "It must be run again, we must have it again."

"All right," answered the hedgehog. "I don't mind, we'll run as often as you like."

So the hare ran seventy-three times more, and the hedgehog always had the best of it. Every time the hare reached either the top or bottom, either the hedgehog or his wife said, "Here I am already!"

The seventy-fourth time, however, the hare could no longer reach the end. In the middle of the field he fell to the ground, and he lay exhausted on the spot. So the hedgehog took the golden turnip which he had won, called his wife out of the furrow, and both went home together in great delight, and if they are not dead, they are living there still.

The Straw Ox

The Straw Ox

NCE upon a time there lived an old man and his wife, and one day she said to him: "Make me a straw ox and smear him over with pitch."

And he asked: "What for?"

And she answered: "Do what I tell you! Never mind what it's for —that's my business!"

So the old man made a straw ox and smeared him over with pitch. Then his wife got ready in the early morning and drove the ox to pasture. She sat down under a tree, and began spinning flax and saying to herself: "Feed, feed, ox, on the fresh green grass. Feed, feed, ox, on the fresh green grass!"

And she went on spinning and spinning, and fell asleep.

Suddenly from out of the thick wood, from out of the dark forest, a bear came running, and ran right up against the ox.

"Who in the world are you?" he asked.

And the ox answered, "I'm the three-year-old ox, all made of straw and smeared over with pitch."

Then the bear said, "Well, if you're smeared over with pitch, give me some to put on my poor torn side."

And the ox answered, "Take some!"

So the bear seized hold of the ox, when, lo and behold! his paw stuck in the pitch. And when he tried to free it with the other paw, that one stuck too. Then he started gnawing with his teeth, and they stuck too. He couldn't tear himself away anyhow. And the old woman woke up and saw the bear stuck fast to the ox.

So she ran home and shouted to her husband: "Come along quickly, a bear has stuck fast to our ox; hurry up and catch him!"

Then his wife got ready in the early morning and drove the ox to pasture.

And he came along, took the bear, led him home, and shut him up in the lumber room.

The next day, as soon as the sun rose, the old woman again drove the ox to pasture, and she herself sat down under a tree, and began spinning flax and saying to herself: "Feed, feed, ox, on the fresh green grass of the field! Feed, feed, ox, on the fresh green grass of the field!"

And she went on spinning and spinning, and fell asleep.

Suddenly from out of the thick wood, from out of the dark forest, a wolf came running, and ran right up against the ox.

"Who in the world are you?" he asked.

And the ox answered, "I'm the three-year-old ox, all made of straw and smeared over with pitch."

Then the wolf said, "Well, if that's so, give me some pitch to put on my poor torn side."

And the ox answered, "By all means!"

So the wolf tried to take some pitch, when, lo and behold! his paw stuck in it. And when he tried to free it, it stuck all the faster. And the old woman woke up and saw the wolf sticking to the ox!

So she ran to fetch her husband, and said, "Come as quickly as you can, there's a wolf stuck to the ox!"

And he came and caught the wolf and put him in the cellar.

The next day, before even the sun had risen, the old woman again drove the ox to pasture, and she herself sat down under a tree, and began spinning flax and saying to herself: "Feed, feed, ox, on the fresh green grass! Feed, feed, ox, on the fresh green grass!"

And she went on spinning and spinning, and fell asleep.

Suddenly from out of the thick wood, from out of the dark forest, a fox came running, and ran right up against the ox.

"What sort of beast are you?" he asked.

And the ox answered, "I'm the three-year-old ox.

all made of straw and smeared over with pitch."

Then the fox said, "Well, then, give me some pitch to rub on my side."

And the fox was just going to take some pitch, when he stuck fast and couldn't free himself. And the old woman woke up and saw the fox sticking to the ox. So she ran to fetch her husband, and he came and took the fox and put him in the cellar as well.

The next day the old woman again sat down under the tree to spin her flax, while the ox fed, and she began spinning and saying to herself: "Feed, feed, ox, on the fresh green grass! Feed, feed, ox, on the fresh green grass!"

And she went on spinning and spinning and fell asleep.

Suddenly from out of the thick wood, from out of

the dark forest, a gray hare came running and ran right up against the ox.

"What sort of beast are you?" he asked.

"I'm the three-year-old ox, all made of straw and smeared over with pitch."

Then the hare said: "Well, then, give me some pitch to rub on my side."

"Take some!" answered the ox.

And the hare caught hold of him with his teeth and, lo and behold! his teeth stuck fast. He tore and tore, but couldn't tear them free. And the old woman woke up, and ran to fetch her husband, and said: "Come as quickly as you can, there's a hare stuck to the ox!"

And the old man came, took the hare, and flung him into the cellar.

Then the old man began to grind his knife, and the bear heard him and asked, "What are you grinding your knife for?"

And he answered, "I'm grinding my knife to take the skin off your back and make myself a fur coat out of it."

But the bear said, "Oh, don't take the skin off my back! Better let me go free and I'll repay you handsomely."

"Well, mind you do!" answered the old man, and so he let the bear go free, and he ran off into the forest.

The next day the old man again began to grind his knife outside the cellar, and the wolf asked him, "What are you grinding your knife for?"

And he answered, "I'm grinding my knife to take the skin off your back and make myself a fur coat out of it."

But the wolf said, "Oh, don't take the skin off my back! Better let me go free and I'll repay you handsomely."

"Well, mind you do!" answered the old man, and so he let the wolf too go free.

Next day he began to grind his knife outside the cellar, and the fox asked him, "What are you grinding your knife for?"

And he answered, "I'm grinding my knife to take the skin off your back, and make myself out of it a collar for my fur coat."

But the fox said, "Oh, don't take the skin off my my back! Better let me go free, and I'll repay you handsomely."

"Well, mind you do!" answered he.

Then the hare was left all alone. And again the old man began to grind his knife, and the hare asked him, "What are you grinding your knife for?"

And he answered, "I'm grinding my knife to take the skin off your back, and make myself some fur gloves out of it."

But the hare said, "Oh, don't take the skin off my

back! Better let me go free and I'll repay you hand-somely."

"Well, mind you do!" he answered, and let the hare too go free.

Early the next morning the old man heard some one knocking at the gate, so he asked, "Who's there?"

And the answer came: "It's I, the bear, come to pay you my debt."

And the old man opened the gate, and there was the bear with a hive of honey he had brought.

So the old man took the honey, when again he heard knock-knock at the gate! "Who's there?" he asked.

And the answer came: "It's I, the wolf, come to pay you my debt."

And there was the wolf with a whole flock of sheep he had driven up.

So the old man let the sheep into the yard, when again he heard knock-knock at the gate.

"Who's there?" he asked.

And the answer came: "It's I, the fox, come to pay you my debt."

And there was the fox with a whole farm-yard full of cocks and hens, and ducks and geese.

Suddenly there came another knock-knock at the gate.

"Who's there?" asked the old man.

And the answer came: It's I, the hare, come to pay you my debt."

And he had brought with him a whole heap of cabbages.

So the old man and his wife lived happily together, and always spoke well and kindly of those beasts.

The Wonderful Pot

The Wonderful Pot

ONCE upon a time a man and his wife lived in a very small cottage. They were very poor, and often wanted for their daily bread. Somehow or other they had managed to keep an only cow, but had been obliged to sell nearly everything else that they had. At length they decided that the cow, too, must go, and the man led her away, intending to bring her to market. As he walked along the road a stranger approached and hailed him, asking if he intended to sell the animal, and how much he could take for it.

"I think," answered he, "that twenty dollars would be a fair price."

"Money I cannot give you," resumed the stranger, "but I have something which is worth as much as twenty dollars. Here is a pot which I am willing to give for your cow." Saying this, he pulled forth an iron pot with three legs and a handle.

"A pot!" exclaimed the cow's owner. "What use would that do me when I have nothing to put in it? My wife and children cannot eat an iron pot. No; money is what I need, and what I must have."

The two men stood still a moment looking at each other and at the cow and the pot, when suddenly the three-legged being began to speak. "Just take me," it said. When the poor man heard this he thought that if it could speak no doubt it could do more than that. So he closed the bargain, received the pot, and returned home with it.

When he reached the cottage he first went to the stall where the cow had been standing, for he did not dare to appear before his wife at once. Having tied the pot to the manger, he went into the room, asking

94

for something to eat, as he was hungry from his long walk.

"Well," said his wife, "did you get a good price for the cow?"

"Yes," he said, "the price was fair enough."

"That is well," returned she. "The money will help us for a long time."

"No," said he, again, "I received no money for the cow."

"Dear me!" cried she, "What did you receive, then?"

He told her to go and look in the stall.

As soon as the woman learned that the three-legged pot was all that had been paid him for the cow, she scolded and said, "I wish I had myself taken the

95

cow to market! I never heard of such foolishness!"
Thus she went on for a while.

"Clean me and put me on the fire," suddenly shouted the pot.

The woman opened her eyes in great wonder, and now it was her turn to think that if the pot could talk no doubt it could do more than this. She cleaned and washed it carefully, and put it on the fire.

"I skip, I skip!" cried the pot.

"How far do you skip?" asked the woman.

"To the rich man's house, to the rich man's house!" it cried again, running from the fireplace to the door, across the yard, and up the road, as fast as the three short legs could carry it. The rich man lived not far away. His wife was baking bread when the pot came running in and jumped up on the table, where it remained standing quite still.

"Ah!" exclaimed the woman, "isn't it wonderful! I just needed you for a pudding which must be baked at once."

Then she heaped a great many good things into the pot—flour, sugar, butter, raisins, spices, almonds, and so on. The pot received it all with a good will. At length the pudding was made, but when the rich man's wife reached for it, intending to put it on the stove, tap, tap, tap, went the three short legs, and the pot stood on the threshold of the open door.

"Dear me, where are you going with my pudding?" cried the woman.

"To the poor man's house," replied the pot, running down the road at great speed.

When the poor people saw the pot coming back and found the pudding, they rejoiced, and the man lost no time in asking his wife whether the bargain did not seem to be an excellent one after all. Yes, she was quite pleased and contented.

Next morning the pot again cried: "I skip, I skip!"

"How far do you skip?" asked they.

"To the rich man's barn!" it shouted, running up the road. When it arrived at the barn it stopped in the door.

"Look at that black pot!" cried the men who were threshing wheat. "Let us see how much it will hold."

They poured a bushel of wheat into it, but it did not seem to fill rapidly. Another bushel went in, but there was still room. Now every grain of wheat went into the pot, but still it seemed capable of holding more. As there was no more wheat to be found, the three short legs began to move, and when the men looked around the pot had reached the gate.

"Stop, stop!" called they. "Where do you go with our wheat?"

"To the poor man's house," replied the pot, speeding down the road and leaving the men behind, dismayed and dumbfounded.

The poor people were delighted when they received wheat enough to feed them for several years.

On the third morning the pot again skipped up the road. It was a beautiful day. The sun shone so brightly that the rich man had spread his money on a table near the open window to prevent his gold from becoming mouldy. All at once the pot stood on the table before him. He began to count his money over, as wealthy men sometimes like to do, and although he could not imagine where this black pot had come from,

he thought it would be a good place to keep his money in the future. So he threw in one handful after another until it held all. At the same moment the pot made a jump from the table to the window-sill.

"Wait!" shouted he. "Where do you go with all my money?"

"To the poor man's house," returned the pot, skipping down the road until the money jumped within it. In the middle of the floor in the poor man's hut it stopped, making its owners cry out in rapture over the unexpected treasure.

"Clean and wash me," said the pot, "and put me aside."

Next morning it again announced that it was ready to skip.

"How far do you skip?" asked they.

"To the rich man's house!"

So it ran up the road again, never stopping until it had reached the wealthy people's kitchen. The man happened to be there himself this time, and as soon as he saw it he cried: "That is the pot which carried

In the middle of the floor in the poor man's hut it stopped.

away our pudding, our wheat, and all our money! I shall make it return what it carried off." He flung himself upon it, but found that he was unable to get off again.

"I skip, I skip!" shouted the pot.

"Skip to the north pole, if you wish!" shouted the man, furiously, trying in vain to free himself.

The three short legs at once moved on, carrying him rapidly down the road. The poor people saw it pass their door, but it never thought of stopping. For all that I know, it went straight to the north pole with its burden.

The poor people became wealthy, and often thought of the wonderful pot with the three short legs which skipped so cheerfully for their good. It was gone, however, and they have never seen it since it carried the rich man towards the north pole.

The Jackal and the Alligator

ONCE upon a time a hungry Jackal went down to the river side in search of little crabs, bits of fish, and whatever else he could find for his dinner. Now it chanced that in this river there lived a great big Alligator, who, being also very hungry, would have been extremely glad to eat the Jackal.

The Jackal ran up and down, here and there, but for a long time could find nothing to eat. At last, close to where the Alligator was lying, among some tall bulrushes under the clear shallow water, he saw a little crab sidling along as fast as his legs could carry him.

The Jackal was so hungry that when he saw this he poked his paw into the water to try and catch the crab, when snap! the old Alligator caught hold of him.

"Oh, dear!" thought the Jackal to himself, "what can I do? This great big Alligator has caught my paw in his mouth, and in another minute he will drag me down under the water and eat me. My only chance is to make him think he has made a mistake."

So he called out in a cheerful voice: "Clever Alligator, clever Alligator, to catch hold of a bulrush root instead of my paw! I hope you will find it very tender."

The Alligator who was so buried among the bulrushes that he could hardly see, thought, on hearing this: "Dear me, how tiresome! I fancied I had caught hold of the Jackal's paw; but there he is, calling out in a cheerful voice; I suppose I must have seized a bulrushroot instead, as he says." And he let the Jackal go.

The Jackal ran away as fast as he could, crying: "Oh, wise Alligator, wise Alligator. So you let me go again!"

Then the Alligator was very vexed, but the Jackal had run away too far to be caught.

Next day the Jackal returned to the river side to get his dinner as before, but because he was very much afraid of the Alligator, he called out: "Whenever I go to look for my dinner, I see the nice little crabs peeping up through the mud; then I catch them and eat them. I wish I could see one now."

The Alligator, who was buried in mud at the bottom of the river, heard every word. So he popped the little point of his snout above the water, thinking: "If I but just show the tip of my nose, the Jackal will take me for a crab, and put in his paw to catch me, and as soon as ever he does I'll gobble him up."

But no sooner did the Jackal see the little tip of the Alligator's nose than he called out: "Aha, my friend, there you are. No dinner for me in this part of the river, then, I think."

And so saying, he ran further on, and fished for his dinner a long way from that place.

The Alligator was very angry at missing the little Jackal a second time, and determined not to let him escape again. So on the following day, when the Jackal returned to the waterside, the Alligator hid himself close to the bank in order to catch him if he could. Now the Jackal was rather afraid of going near the river, for he thought: "Perhaps this Alligator will catch me to-day." But yet, being hungry, he did not wish to go without his dinner, so to make all as safe as he could, he cried: "Where are all the little crabs gone? There is not one here, and I am so hungry, and generally, even when they are under the water, one can see them going bubble, bubble, bubble! and all the little bubbles go pop! pop! pop!"

On hearing this the Alligator, who was buried in the mud under the river bank, thought: "I will pretend to be a little crab." And he began to blow, "Puff, puff, puff! Bubble, bubble, bubble!" All the great big bubbles rushed to the surface of the river and burst there and the Jackal saw very well who must be there, and ran away as fast as he could, saying: "Thank you, kind Alligator, thank you, thank you. Indeed I would not have come here had I known you were so close."

The Alligator was quite cross to think of being so often deceived by a little Jackal, and he said to himself: "I will not be tricked again. Next time I will be very cunning."

So for a long time he waited and waited for the Jackal to return to the riverside. But the Jackal did not come, for he had thought to himself: "If matters

go on in this way I shall some day be caught and eaten by the wicked old Alligator. I had better content myself with living on wild figs." And he went no more near the river, but stayed in the jungle and ate wild figs, and roots which he dug out with his paws.

When the Alligator found this out he determined to try to catch the Jackal on land, so going under the largest of the wild fig trees, where the ground was covered with the fallen fruit, he collected a quantity of it together, and burying himself under the great heap,

111

waited for the Jackal to appear. But no sooner did the cunning little animal see this great heap of wild figs all collected together than he thought: "That looks very like my friend the Alligator." And to discover if it was so or not he called out: "The juicy little figs that I love to eat always tumble down from the tree, and roll here and there as the wind drives them. But this great heap of figs is quite still; these cannot be good figs. I will not eat any of them."

"Ho, ho!" thought the Alligator; "is that all? How suspicious that Jackal is! I will make the figs roll about a little, and then, when he sees that, he will doubtless come and eat them."

So the great beast shook himself, and all the heap of little figs went roll, roll, roll; some a mile this way, some a mile that, farther than they had ever rolled before, or than the blustering wind could have driven them!

Seeing this the Jackal scampered away, saying: "I am obliged to you, Alligator, for letting me know you were there, for indeed I should hardly have guessed it. You were so buried under that heap of figs."

The Alligator, hearing this, was so angry that he ran after the Jackal, but the latter ran away very, very fast, too quickly to be caught. Then the Alligator said to himself: "I will not allow that little wretch to make fun of me another time, and then run away out of reach. I will show him that I can be more cunning than he fancies." So early the next morning he crawled as fast as he could to the Jackal's house, crept into it, and hid himself, waiting for the Jackal, who was out, to return home.

But when the Jackal got near the place, he looked about him, and thought: "Dear me, the ground looks as if some heavy creature had been walking over it, and here are great clods of earth knocked down from each side of the door of my house as if a very big animal had been trying to squeeze himself through it. I certainly will not go inside until I know that all is safe there."

So he called out: "Little house, pretty house, my sweet little house, why do you not give an answer when I call? If I come, and all is safe and right, you always call out to me. Is anything wrong that you do not speak?"

113

Then the Alligator, who was inside, thought: "If that is the case I had better call out, that he may fancy all is right in his house." And in as gentle a voice as he could, he said: "Sweet little Jackal."

At hearing these words the Jackal felt quite frightened, and thought to himself: "So the dreadful Alligator is there! I must to do away with him, if I can, for if I do not he will certainly catch me some day."

He therefore answered: "Thank you, my dear little house. I like to hear your pretty voice. I am coming in a minute, but first I must collect firewood to cook my dinner." And he ran as fast as he could, and dragged all the dry branches and bits of stick he could find close up to the mouth of the house.

Meanwhile the Alligator inside kept as quiet as a

mouse; but he could not help laughing a little to himself, as he thought: "So I have deceived this tiresome little Jackal at last. In a few minutes he will run in here, and then won't I snap him up!"

When the Jackal had gathered together all the sticks he could find, and put them round the door of his house, he set them on fire, and pushed them as far into it as possible. There was such a quantity of them that they soon blazed up into a great fire, and the smoke and flames filled the house and smothered the wicked old Alligator. And the little Jackal was never bothered again.

Mother Hulda

A WIDOW had two daughters; one was pretty and industrious, the other was lazy and ugly.

As she loved the ugly one the better, the pretty one was made to do all the work, and be the drudge of the house. Every day the poor girl had to sit by a well on the high road and spin until her fingers ached. Now it happened once that the spindle slipped out of her hand and fell in the well. Then she began to cry, and ran to her mother, and told her of her misfortune; and her mother scolded her without mercy, and said:

"As you have let the spindle fall in, you must go and fetch it out again!" So she did.

At the bottom of the well, she found a beautiful meadow, and the sun was shining on all the flowers that grew round her. She walked on through the meadow until she came to an oven that was full of bread.

The bread called out to her:

"Oh, take me out, take me out, or I shall burn; I am baked enough already!"

Then she opened the oven door and took out the loaves. And she went farther on till she came to a tree weighed down with apples, and it called out to her:

"Oh, shake me, shake me, we apples are all of us ripe!"

Then she shook the tree until the apples fell like rain, and she shook until there were no more to fall; and when she had gathered them together in a heap, she went on farther.

At last she came to a little house, in which there lived an old woman.

120

At last she came to a little house, in which there lived an old woman.

"Come and live with me," said the woman, "and if you do the housework well and in orderly fashion, things shall go well with you. You must take great

pains to make my bed well, and shake it up thoroughly, so that the feathers fly about. When you do that, it snows in the world, for I am Mother Hulda."

As the old woman spoke so kindly, the girl took courage, consented, and went to work. She did everything to the old woman's satisfaction, and shook the bed with such a will that the feathers flew about like snowflakes. And so she led a good life, had never a cross word, but boiled and roasted meat every day. When she had lived a long time with Mother Hulda, she began to feel sad, not knowing herself what ailed her; at last she began to think she must be homesick;

121

and although she was a thousand times better off where she was, yet she had a great longing to go home. At last she said to her mistress,

"I am homesick, and although I am very well off here, I cannot stay any longer; I must go back to my own home."

Mother Hulda answered, "It pleases me well that you should wish to go home, and, as you have served me faithfully, I will undertake to send you there!"

She took her by the hand and led her to a large door standing open. As she was passing through it there fell upon her a heavy shower of gold. The gold hung all about her, so that she was covered with it.

"All this is yours, because you have been so industrious," said Mother Hulda; and, besides that, she gave her the spindle she had dropped into the well. Then the door was shut again, and the girl found her-

self back again in the world, not far from her mother's house; and as she passed through the yard the cock stood on the top of the well and cried,

"Cock-a-doodle doo!
Our golden girl has come home too!"

Then she went in to her mother, and as she had returned covered with gold she was well received.

The girl told everything that had happened to her, and when the mother heard how she came to have such great riches she began to wish that her ugly and idle daughter might have the same good fortune. So she sent her to sit by the well and spin. She threw her spindle into the well, and jumped in herself. She found herself, like her sister, in the beautiful meadow, and followed the same path, and when she came to the oven, the bread cried out,

"Oh, take me out, take me out, or I shall burn; I am quite done already!"

But she answered, "That is all very fine; suppose one of you should fall on my head," and went on farther.

When she came to Mother Hulda's house, she entered into her service at once. The first day she put her hand well to the work, and was industrious, and did everything Mother Hulda bade her, because of the gold she expected; but the second day she began to be

idle, and the third day still more so, so that she would not get up in the morning. Neither did she make Mother Hulda's bed as it ought to have been made, and did not shake it for the feathers to fly about.

Mother Hulda soon grew tired of her, and gave her warning, at which the lazy girl was well pleased, and thought that now the shower of gold was coming. Mother Hulda led her to the door, and as she stood in the doorway, instead of the shower of gold a great kettle full of pitch was emptied over her.

"That is the reward for your service," said Mother Hulda, and shut the door. So the lazy girl came home all covered with pitch, and the cock on the top of the well seeing her, cried,

"Cock-a-doodle-doo!
Our dirty girl has come home too!"

And the pitch remained sticking to her fast, and never, as long as she lived, could it be got off.

Hans in Luck

ANS had served his master seven years, and at the end of the seventh year he said, "Master, my time is up. I want to go home and see my mother; so give me my wages."

"You have served me truly and faithfully," said the master. "As the service is, so must the wages be." And he gave him a lump of gold as big as his head. Hans pulled his handkerchief out of his pocket and tied up the lump of gold in it, hoisted it on his shoulder, and set off on his way home. As he was trudging along, there came in sight a man riding on a spirited horse, and looking very gay and lively.

"Oh," cried Hans aloud, "how splendid riding must be, sitting at one's ease as in an armchair, stumbling over no stones, and saving one's shoes.

The horseman heard Hans say this, and called out to him, "Well, Hans, what are you doing on foot?"

"I can't help myself," said Hans. "I have this great

lump to carry; to be sure it is gold, but then I can't hold my head straight, and it hurts my shoulder."

"I'll tell you what," said the horseman, "we will change; I will give you my horse, and you shall give me your lump of gold."

"With all my heart," said Hans; "but I warn you, you will find it heavy." The horseman got down, took the gold, and, helping Hans up, he gave the reins into his hand.

"When you want to go fast," said he, "you must click your tongue and cry, 'Gee-up!'"

Hans, as he sat upon his horse, was glad at heart, and rode off with merry cheer. After a while he thought he should like to go quicker, so he began to click with his tongue and to cry, "Gee-up!"

Then the horse began to trot, and Hans was thrown before he knew what was going to happen. There he lay in the ditch by the side of the road. The horse would have got away but he was caught by a peasant who was passing that way driving a cow before him. Hans pulled himself together and got upon his feet, feeling very vexed. "Poor work, riding," said he, "especially on a horse like this, who

And the horse began to trot . . . . .

starts off and throws you before you know where you are, going near to break your neck; never shall I try that game again; now, your cow is something worth having, one can jog on comfortably after her and have her milk, butter and cheese every day into the bargain. What would I not give to have such a cow!"

"Well, now," said the peasant, "since it will be doing you such a favor, I don't mind exchanging my cow for your horse."

Hans agreed most joyfully, and the peasant, swinging himself into the saddle, was soon out of sight.

Hans went along driving his cow quietly before him, and thinking all the while of the fine bargain he had made.

"With only a piece of bread I shall have everything I can possibly want, for I shall always be able to have butter and cheese with it, and if I am thirsty I have nothing to do but to milk my cow; and what more is there for heart to wish!"

When he came to an inn he made a halt, and in the joy of his heart ate up all the food he had brought with him, dinner and supper and all, and bought half a glass of beer with his last two farthings. Then on he went again driving his cow until he should come to the village where his mother lived. It was now the middle of the day, and the sun grew hotter and hotter. Hans found himself on a heath which would require an hour's journey to cross. He began to feel very hot, and so thirsty that his tongue clove to the roof of his mouth.

"Never mind," said Hans, "I can find a remedy. I will milk my cow at once." Tying her to a dry tree, and taking off his leather cap to serve for a pail, he began to milk, but not a drop came. As he set to work rather awkwardly, the impatient beast gave him such a kick on the head with her hind foot that he fell to the ground. For some time he could not think

132

where he was, when luckily there came by a butcher who was wheeling along a young pig in a wheelbarrow.

"Here's a fine piece of work!" cried he, helping poor Hans on his legs again.

Then Hans related to him all that had happened; and the butcher handed him a cup, saying, "Here, take a drink, and be a man again; of course the cow would give no milk; she is old and only fit to draw burdens, or to be slaughtered."

"Well, to be sure," said Hans scratching his head. "Who would have thought it? Of course it is a very handy way of getting meat when a man has a beast of his own to kill; but for my part I do not care much about cow beef; it is rather tasteless. Now, if I had but a young pig, that is much better meat, and then the sausages!"

"Look here, Hans," said the butcher, "just for love of you I will exchange, and will give you my pig instead of your cow."

"Heaven reward such kindness!" cried Hans, and handing over the cow, received in exchange the pig.

On went Hans, thinking how everything turned out according to his wishes, and how, if trouble overtook him, all was sure to be set right directly. After a while he fell in with a peasant, who was carrying a fine white goose under his arm. They bade each other

good-day, and Hans began to tell about his luck, and how he had made so many good exchanges. The peasant told him that he was taking the goose to a christening feast.

"Just feel how heavy it is," said he, taking it up by the wings; "it has been fattening for the last eight weeks; and when it is roasted, won't the fat run down!"

"Yes, indeed," said Hans, weighing it in his hand, "very fine to be sure; but my pig is not to be despised."

Upon which the peasant glanced cautiously on all sides and shook his head.

"I am afraid," said he, "that there is something not quite right about your pig. In the village I have just left one had actually been stolen from the bailiff's yard. I fear, I fear you have it in your hand; they have sent after the thief, and it would be a bad lookout for you if it was found with you."

Poor Hans grew pale with fright. "For Heaven's sake," said he, "help me out of this scrape. I am a stranger in these parts; take my pig and give me your goose."

"It will be running some risk," said the man, "but I will do it sooner than that you should come to grief."

So, taking the cord in his hand, he drove the pig quickly along a by-path, and lucky Hans went on his way home with the goose under his arm.

"The more I think of it," said he to himself, "the better the bargain seems; first I get the roast goose,

135

then the fat; that will last for a whole year for bread and dripping; and lastly the beautiful white feathers, which I can stuff my pillow with; how comfortably I shall sleep upon it, and how pleased my mother will be!"

When he reached the last village, he saw a knife-grinder with his barrow; his wheel went whirring round, and he sang,

"My scissors I grind, and my wheel I turn;
And all good fellows my trade should learn,
For all that I meet with just serves my turn."

Hans stood and looked at him; and at last he spoke to him and said, "You seem very well off, and merry with your grinding."

"Yes," answered the knife-grinder, "my handiwork pays very well. I call a man a good grinder who, every time he puts his hand in his pocket finds money there. But where did you buy that fine goose?"

"I did not buy it, but I exchanged my pig for it," said Hans.

"And the pig?"

"I exchanged my cow for it."

"And the cow?"

"I exchanged my horse for it."

"And the horse?"

"I gave for the horse a lump of gold as big as my head."

"And the gold?"

"Oh, that was my wage for seven years' service."

"You seem to have fended for yourself very well," said the knife-grinder. "Now, if you could but manage to have money in your pocket every time you put your hand in, your fortune is made."

"How shall I manage that?" said Hans.

"You must be a knife-grinder like me," said the man. "All you want is a grindstone, the rest comes of itself. I have one here; to be sure, it is a little damaged, but I don't mind letting you have it in exchange for your goose; what say you?"

"How can you ask?" answered Hans. "I shall be the luckiest fellow in the world, for if I find money whenever I put my hand in my pocket, there is nothing more left to want."

So he handed over the goose to the man and received the grindstone in exchange.

"Now," said the knife-grinder, taking up a heavy common stone that lay near him, "here is another proper sort of stone that will stand a good deal of wear and that you can hammer out your old nails upon. Take it with you, and carry it carefully."

Hans lifted up the stone and carried it off with a contented mind. "I must have been born under a lucky star!" cried he, while his eyes sparkled for joy. "I have only to wish for a thing and it is mine."

After a while he began to feel rather tired, as he had been on his legs since daybreak; he also began to feel rather hungry, as in the fullness of his joy at getting the cow, he had eaten up all he had. At last he could scarcely go on at all, and had to make a stop every moment, for the stones weighed him down most unmercifully, and he could not help wishing that he did not feel obliged to drag them along.

On he went at a snail's pace until he came to a
well; then he thought he would rest and take a drink
of the fresh water. He placed the stones carefully
by his side at the edge of the well; then he sat down.
As he stooped to drink, he happened to give the
stones a little push, and they both fell into the water

with a splash. Then Hans, having watched them
disappear, jumped for joy, and thanked his stars that
he had been so lucky as to get rid of the stones that
had weighed upon him so long without any effort of
his own.

"I really think," cried he, "I am the luckiest man
under the sun."

So he went, without a care, until he reached his
mother's house.

The Frog Prince

The Frog Prince

IN the good old times when it was still of some use to wish for the thing one wanted, there lived a King whose daughters were very beautiful, but the youngest was so lovely that the sun himself, who had seen so much, wondered at her beauty, each time he looked at her.

Near the royal castle there was a great dark wood, and in the wood under an old linden tree was a well. When the day was hot, the King's daughter used to go into the wood and sit by the edge of the cool well; and if the time seemed long, she would take out a golden ball and toss it up and catch it again. This was her favorite pastime.

It happened one day that the golden ball, instead of falling back into the maiden's little hand, dropped to the ground near the edge of the well and rolled in.

The King's daughter followed it with her eyes as it sank, but the well was deep, so deep that the bottom could not be seen. Then she began to weep, and she wept and wept, as if she could never be comforted.

While she was thus weeping she heard a voice saying to her:

"What is the matter, King's daughter? Your tears would melt a heart of stone."

When she looked to see where the voice came from, she saw a frog stretching his thick ugly head out of the water.

"Oh, is it you, old waddler?" she said. "I weep because my golden ball has fallen into the well."

"Never mind, do not weep," answered the frog. "I can help you; but what will you give me if I bring back your golden ball to you?"

"Whatever you like, dear frog," said she, "my clothes, my pearls and jewels, or even the golden crown that I wear."

"Your clothes, your pearls, your jewels and your golden crown are not for me," answered the frog, "but if you would love me, and have me for your companion and playfellow, and let me sit by you at the table, and eat from your plate, and drink from your cup, and sleep in your little bed,—if you will promise all this, then I would dive under the water and bring your golden ball to you."

"Oh, yes," she answered, "I will promise all, whatever you want, if you will only bring me back my golden ball."

She thought to herself: "What nonsense he talks As if he could do anything but sit in the water and croak with the other frogs, or could be anyone's companion!"

But the frog, as soon as he had heard her promise, drew his head under the water and sank down out of sight. In a little while he came up again with the ball in his mouth, and he threw it on the grass.

The King's daughter was overjoyed to see her plaything again, and she caught it up and ran off with it.

"Stop, stop!" cried the frog. "Take me up too; I cannot run as fast as you."

But it was of no use, for croak as loud as he might, she would not listen to him, but ran quickly home, and very soon forgot all about the poor frog, who had to plunge again to the bottom of the well.

The next day when the King's daughter was sitting at the table with the King and all the court, eating from her golden plate, there came a sound of something creeping up the marble steps, pitter patter. Then there came a knocking at the door, and a voice cried:

"Youngest King's daughter, let me in!"

She ran to see who it could be, but when she opened the door and saw the frog sitting outside, she quickly

146

closed the door again and went back to the table, feeling very uneasy.

The King noticed how quickly her heart was beating and said:

"My child, what are you afraid of? Is there a giant standing at the door ready to carry you off?"

"Oh, no!" said she; "not a giant but a horrid frog."

"And what does the frog want?" asked the King.

"Oh, dear father," answered she, "when I was sitting by the well yesterday, playing with my golden ball, it fell into the water, and while I was crying because I had lost it, the frog came up and promised to bring it back to me if I would let him be my companion. I never thought that he would leave the water and come after me; but now he is outside the door and he wants to come in to me."

Then the frog knocked a second time and cried:
>"Youngest King's daughter,
>Open to me;
>By the well water
>What promised you me?
>Youngest King's daughter,
>Now open to me."

Then the King said, "That which you promised you must perform; so go now and let him in."

So she opened the door and the frog hopped in following at her heels till she reached her chair.

Then he cried:

"Lift me up to you on the table."

She refused until her father told her to do it.

When the frog was on the table, he said, "Now push your golden plate a little nearer, so that we may eat together."

She did as he asked, but everyone could see that she did so unwillingly.

The frog greatly enjoyed the meal, but every morsel the Princess ate seemed to stick in her throat.

At last the frog said, "I have had enough now, and as I am very tired, you must carry me up to your room and put me in your silken bed, that I may go to sleep."

Then the King's daughter began to weep, because she did not want the cold frog to sleep in her little bed.

But the King said firmly, "What you promised you must perform."

So she picked him up with her finger and thumb, and carried him upstairs and placed him in a corner.

But he said: "I am tired and want to sleep; put me in your silken bed."

The Princess most ungraciously did so, crying, "Now will you be quiet, you horrid frog?"

At that he ceased to be a frog and all at once became a charming Prince with beautiful kind eyes.

Then he told her how a wicked witch had turned him into a frog and that no one but a King's daughter could release him from his enchantment.

It came to pass that, with her father's consent, the Princess married the Prince, and their wedding was celebrated with great joy throughout the Kingdom.